W9-DDP-252

DATE DUE

Hispanic Heritage

Hispanic Heritage

Title List

Central American Immigrants to the United States: Refugees from Unrest

Cuban Americans: Exiles from an Island Home

First Encounters Between Spain and the Americas: Two Worlds Meet

Latino Americans and Immigration Laws: Crossing the Border

Latino Americans in Sports, Film, Music, and Government: Trailblazers

Latino Arts and Their Influence on the United States: Songs, Dreams, and Dances

Latino Cuisine and Its Influence on American Foods: The Taste of Celebration

Latino Economics in the United States: Job Diversity

Latino Folklore and Culture: Stories of Family, Traditions of Pride

Latino Migrant Workers: America's Harvesters

Latinos Today: Facts and Figures

The Latino Religious Experience: People of Faith and Vision

Mexican Americans' Role in the United States: A History of Pride, A Future of Hope

Puerto Ricans' History and Promise: Americans Who Cannot Vote

South America's Immigrants to the United States: The Flight from Turmoil

The Story of Latino Civil Rights: Fighting for Justice

Latino Migrant Workers

America's Harvesters

by Christopher Hovius

Mason Crest Publishers

Philadelphia

Mason Crest Publishers Inc.

370 Reed Road

Broomall, Pennsylvania 19008

(866) MCP-BOOK (toll free)

First printing

1 2 3 4 5 6 7 8 9 10

Library of Congress Cataloging-in-Publication Data

Hovius, Christopher.

Latino migrant workers : America's harvesters / by Christopher Hovius.

p. cm. — (Hispanic heritage)

Includes index.

ISBN 1-59084-937-X   ISBN 1-59084-924-8 (series)

1. Migrant agricultural laborers—United States—Juvenile literature. 2. Alien labor, Latin American—Juvenile literature. 3. Latin Americans—Juvenile literature. I. Title. II. Hispanic heritage (Philadelphia, Pa.)

HD1525.H69 2005

331.5'44'08968073—dc22

2004018231

Produced by Harding House Publishing Service, Inc., Vestal, NY.

Interior design by Dianne Hodack and MK Bassett-Harvey.

Cover design by Dianne Hodack.

Printed in the Hashemite Kingdom of Jordan.

Contents

Introduction

by José E. Limón, Ph.D.

ven before there was a United States, Hispanics were present in what would become this country. Beginning in the sixteenth century, Spanish explorers traversed North America, and their explorations encouraged settlement as early as the sixteenth century in what is now northern New Mexico and Florida, and as late as the mid-eighteenth century in what is now southern Texas and California.

Later, in the nineteenth century, following Spain's gradual withdrawal from the New World, Mexico in particular established its own distinctive presence in what is now the southwestern part of the United States, a presence reinforced in the first half of the twentieth century by substantial immigration from that country. At the close of the nineteenth century, the U.S. war with Spain brought Cuba and Puerto Rico into an interactive relationship with the United States, the latter in a special political and economic affiliation with the United States even as American power influenced the course of almost every other Latin American country.

The books in this series remind us of these historical origins, even as each explores the present reality of different Hispanic groups. Some of these books explore the contemporary social origins—what social scientists call the "push" factors—behind the accelerating Hispanic immigration to America: political instability, economic underdevelopment and crisis, environmental degradation, impoverished or wholly absent educational systems, and other circumstances contribute to many Latin Americans deciding they will be better off in the United States.

And, for the most part, they will be. The vast majority come to work and work very hard, in order to earn better wages than they would back home. They fill significant labor needs in the U.S. economy and contribute to the economy through lower consumer prices and sales taxes.

When they leave their home countries, many immigrants may initially fear that they are leaving behind vital and important aspects of their home cultures: the Spanish language, kinship ties, food, music, folklore, and the arts. But as these books also make clear, culture is a fluid thing, and these native cultures are not only brought to America, they are also replenished in the United States in fascinating and novel ways. These books further suggest to us that Hispanic groups enhance American culture as a whole.

Our country—especially the young, future leaders who will read these books—can only benefit by the fair and full knowledge these authors provide about the socio-historical origins and contemporary cultural manifestations of America's Hispanic heritage.

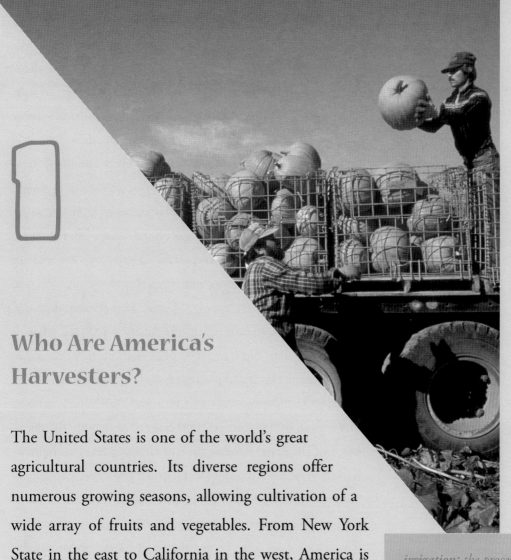

Who Are America's Harvesters?

The United States is one of the world's great agricultural countries. Its diverse regions offer numerous growing seasons, allowing cultivation of a wide array of fruits and vegetables. From New York State in the east to California in the west, America is filled with fertile countryside. Even in the sun-drenched southwestern states, farmers use complicated *irrigation* schemes to cultivate the arid desert plains. The land's richness adorns grocery store aisles with peaches from Georgia, blueberries from Maine, and potatoes from Idaho. Yet in the midst of this abundance, one of America's most impoverished groups struggles to earn a meager existence from the otherwise fertile soil.

irrigation: the process of bringing water to a dry area.

Artwork
Many traditional Latino designs center on farmworkers and their crops.

9

seasonally: based on
the time of the year.

mainstream: the ideas,
actions, and values
most widely accepted by
a society or particular
group.

These men, women, and children are migrant farmworkers. Without their hard, often unrecognized work growing, picking, and packing fruits and vegetables, the foods Americans enjoy every day would never make it onto American tables.

Migrant farmworkers are people who are *seasonally* or temporarily employed in agriculture and who must stay overnight away from their homes because their places of work are so far away. At the beginning of the agricultural season, migrant farmworkers plant and cultivate crops. During harvest season, migrant farmworkers pick the fruits and vegetables in the orchards and fields where they were grown. Migrant farmworkers then dry, package, process, and freeze much of America's produce. Migrant agricultural labor, therefore, takes place both in the fields and in the processing plants and packaging sheds of the country.

The U.S. Departments of Labor and Agriculture estimate that around 800,000 to 900,000 people (or roughly the population of Delaware) work as migrant farmworkers. This estimate is likely very low. According to a Cornell University paper titled "Facts on Farmworkers in the United States," the real number of migrant farmworkers is probably between one and three million. That's more like the population of Maine or Mississippi. Why is there such a big gap between these estimates? Often migrant farmworkers live out of the gaze of *mainstream* society because of severe poverty and, in some cases, because they come from outside the United States and work without proper authorization.

About 81 percent of migrant farmworkers are born outside the United States, and most (about 77 percent) come from Mexico. Many people assume that all migrant workers from other countries are illegal workers, but this is untrue. Many foreign migrant workers are brought to the United States and hired legally. The U.S. Department of Labor has developed a special

Americans depend on migrant workers' labor.

Many of America's vegetables are picked by migrant workers.

labor category for foreign farmworkers: they are considered temporary foreign workers and are granted authorization to work only in agriculture. Authorization usually lasts less than one year and must be continuously renewed. Nevertheless, 52 percent of all migrant farmworkers lack work authorization, meaning that they are working in the country illegally. Many people, including *labor contractors*, workers, and farmers find it easier to operate outside regulations than obtain proper authorization.

A Life of Toil and Insecurity

ou may wonder why so many of America's agricultural workers come from outside the United States. The answer has to do with economics. In the United States, the average American-born worker makes $37,000 each year. The average migrant farmworker, however, makes less than $7,500 a year. Such low wages have created an *epidemic* of poverty among farmworkers. About 46 percent of all farmworkers live below the *poverty line*, compared to just 12 percent of the U.S. population as a whole. In addition to being poorly paid, farmwork is heavy manual labor involving hours bending over in fields, harvesting fruit, and lifting boxes laden with produce. The days stretch twelve and even fifteen hours long, and many of these hours are spent in the hot sun. Migrant farmworkers are usually not guaranteed a day off. Some people complain about foreign farmworkers, saying that they steal jobs from Americans. The truth, however, is that the vast majority of Americans are unwilling to perform this backbreaking labor for such unfair wages, and farm owners (also called growers) find it difficult to fill these jobs with American-born workers. Only the most desperate and poverty-stricken people sacrifice themselves to life as migrant farmworkers, and growers meet the labor shortage by importing workers from other countries.

The low wages migrant farmworkers make today are the result of unprecedented changes in the American agricultural industry. Although the American farmland retains the appearance of an idyllic countryside, a great deal has changed since the days when small family farms were responsible for most agricultural production. Some farms are still owned and operated by families and provide a livelihood for the few people who live year-round and work full-time on the particular farm. Since the end of World War II, however, more farms have begun operating like big businesses. Many farms are even owned by large *corporations* like Dole, Sunrype, and Gallo. Large corporate-owned farms can cover hundreds, even thousands of acres. They grow huge amounts of produce and therefore need a huge number of workers.

labor contractors: people who find, hire, transport, and pay workers for an employer.

epidemic: a fast-moving and widespread outbreak of a disease.

poverty line: a government-established level of income below which someone is considered to be living in poverty.

corporations: a company recognized by law as a single body with its own powers and liabilities, separate from those of the individual owners or members of the board of directors.

Farmworkers Who Stay Put

In this book we will explore the lives of migrant farmworkers, but not all agricultural workers are migrants. In fact, 42 percent of all farmworkers harvest only those crops that grow near their homes. They do not spend the night away from their permanent residence to obtain work and, consequently, are not considered "migrants." During the off season, when work on farms is scarce, these workers find jobs in other industries like construction.

In order to get the workers they need, many growers hire people known as labor contractors. Contractors act as middlemen. They are paid to find workers, hire them, and bring them to the grower. The farmer pays the contractor, and the contractor pays the migrant farmworkers. The more money the contractor can withhold from the farmworkers, the higher profit the contractor will make.

Not only do migrant farmworkers receive low wages for their labor, they have no job security; many do not know if their job will continue from one day to the next. The length of time for which an agricultural worker is hired varies from one day to several weeks. Sometimes people are guaranteed a

Migrant workers go to work when the crops are ready to be harvested.

job picking crops for one particular grower for the entire harvest season. Depending on the crop, this could last for up to six weeks. Workers with jobs like these might even live in labor camps set up on the farm. In other cases, migrant farmworkers struggle daily to find work. Gathering at dawn at a pick-up point, migrants await offers of work. If they find employment, they are driven to the jobsite. At the end of the work day, they are dropped off where they had assembled. Farms that operate with this type of labor are known as day-haul operations. People who work day-haul jobs face serious job insecurity, since each day they must start their job search all over again.

Regardless of whether farmwork is for several weeks or day-haul, layoffs are common. At certain times of the year, a large farm is transformed into a beehive of activity with

What's in a Word?

oday many people use the terms Latino and Hispanic interchangeably, but they are not actually synonymous. Hispanic and Latino are terms for linguistic groups, or groups of people who speak the same language. The term Hispanic refers to people from North, Central, or South America or the Caribbean who speak Spanish or have Spanish heritage. The term Latino refers to people from Central America, South America, or the Caribbean who speak Spanish, French, or Portuguese.

hundreds of workers spread across the sprawling acreage. At other times, the fields are virtually empty. While large farms require the most workers, they also tend to hire these workers in bursts. For example, during harvest season, a grower requires more people to pick the ripening crops. During the off-season, only a small number of hands are needed to tend the fields. Therefore, farmworkers are hired in large numbers for the several weeks during harvest season and then laid off. Most farmworkers spend only short periods of time working for one employer before moving on and seeking work elsewhere.

Map of migrant workers' routes

A Life of Migration

he seasonal nature of the work on large farms and the short periods of employment have created a pattern of migration that defines the lifestyles of migrant farmworkers. The United States has three major migrant "streams," or routes, that migrant laborers follow as crops ripen. Most migrant farm laborers, including those who come from outside the United States, set up "home bases" in California, Texas, or Florida. Then they spend several months of the year on the harvest trail, following the ripening crops northward into the late summer and early fall. A migrant worker who lives in California will travel the coast and move inland to work in the fertile valleys. As the summer progresses, the California-based workers move farther north into Oregon and Washington. When winter comes, they return south to their home base.

*diverse: consisting of
many different things
or elements.*

*multicultural: consist-
ing of different coun-
tries, ethnic groups, or
religions.*

*Latinos: people from
Central America, South
America, or the
Caribbean who speak
Spanish, French, or
Portuguese.*

*Hispanic: people from
North, Central, or
South America or the
Caribbean who speak
Spanish or have
Spanish heritage.*

Similar patterns exist for migrants in Texas and Florida. Migrants from Texas take part in harvests from Washington on the West Coast to states like Ohio and Illinois in the Midwest. Some migrants from this stream also work on farms in southern states like Georgia and the Carolinas. The Florida-based stream generally does not migrate further west than Tennessee. These migrants stream north along the East Coast. As the summer turns to fall, they travel through the southern states, to the Mid-Atlantic states, and on into New England.

Farmworkers' Identity

So who are America's farmworkers, the people on whom we all depend for so much of our food? America is a *diverse* nation, and in many ways migrant workers reflect the *multicultural* patchwork of American society. According to the National Agricultural Workers Survey, some migrant workers are U.S.-born *Latinos*, others U.S.-born white Americans, and still others are U.S.-born black Americans. As we stated earlier, however, most migrant farmworkers come from outside of the United States, especially from Mexico. Today, nine out of ten migrant farmworkers, whether U.S. or foreign born, are

Hispanic. In this book, you will learn specifically about the lives of Latino and Hispanic migrant farmworkers.

Latino farmworkers, whether they come from outside the United States or are American-born, face many challenges. Regardless of the crop they harvest, the work they perform, or the particular group from which they come, farmworkers have helped create the United States and keep food on its tables. Yet these workers remain some of the most impoverished and underappreciated people in America. In the next chapter, we look at the history of migrant farming to understand how this system of agricultural labor came about and what effects it has on America's Latino community today.

Farmworkers face many challenges.

▦abla ▦spañol

Estados Unidos (ace-tah-dohs oo-nee-dohs): United States

finca (feen-cah): farm

agricultura (ah-gree-cool-too-rah): agriculture

comida (co-mee-dah): food

2

Uprooted: The History of Migrant Farming

At one time in American history, migrant farm-work was a rare phenomenon. But the Great Depression changed all that.

foreclosed: to take away a mortgagee's right to live in her home, usually because payments have not been made.

The Great Depression and Its Effects on American Agriculture

In the 1930s, when millions of people were uprooted by the Great Depression and massive droughts, huge numbers of people began migrating in search of farmwork. Triggered by New York City's massive stock market collapse of 1929, the Great Depression reached across all of America. With one in every four people without work, far more people were searching for employment than there were jobs available. As people fell behind on taxes and debts, they took out loans to cover the costs of staying in business and keeping their homes.

Throughout the 1930s, things only got worse. Severe weather disrupted farming. At least four separate droughts ravaged the American plains. High temperatures and insect infestations added misery to the arid landscape. Poor soil conservation stripped nutrients from the earth, reducing moisture content and making the land vulnerable to wind erosion. Dust storms erupted across Oklahoma, Texas, and Arkansas. High winds gathered up the dry, impoverished topsoil and deposited it as far away as New York City. The windswept region became known as the Dustbowl.

No crops meant no money, and no money meant the bank would soon be knocking at the door. Banks *foreclosed* on those unable to repay their loans. Families were torn from the land they had worked and lived on for several generations. As farm after farm went under, families left their land in search of work.

John Steinbeck

John Steinbeck, who lived from 1902 to 1968, was born in the fruit-growing region of Salinas, California. Much of his writing, such as a piece about striking migrant fruit pickers in California, focused on rural laborers and their economic troubles. In 1962, Steinbeck was awarded the Nobel Prize in Literature "for his realistic and imaginative writings, combining as they do sympathetic humour and keen social perception."

It was America's first great migration of farmworkers. During the worst of the Depression, 3.5 million people sought agricultural employment as migrant laborers. John Steinbeck, a young journalist from California, followed the stories of migrants who trailed westward out of the Dustbowl in search of jobs. In 1939, he wrote *The Grapes of Wrath*, a novel that won Steinbeck acclaim as one of America's great writers. In it, Steinbeck chronicles the journey of migrant "Okies," white farmers who were forced from the Dustbowl in search of work in California.

In 1936, Steinbeck's "The Harvest Gypsies," a seven-part series of nonfiction articles, appeared in the *San Francisco News*. In it, he described the living conditions migrants

During the Great Depression, families loaded what they could into ramshackle cars and headed west, looking for work on the farms of California.

faced in California's labor camps. Steinbeck's accounts overflow with descriptions of extreme poverty, disease, death, and starvation. In his vivid accounts, children die from malnutrition, infants are born dead, and medical care is nonexistent. Growers and landowners are uncaring and calloused people dominated by corporations immune to the plight of struggling families. One article recalls, "As one little boy in a squatters' camp said, 'When they need us they call us migrants, and when we've picked their crop, we're bums and we got to get out.' . . . And so they move, frantically, with starvation close behind them."

In an attempt to save the United States from the Great Depression, President Franklin

Delano Roosevelt created an economic plan called the New Deal. Ironically, the agricultural policies included in Roosevelt's plan actually harmed farmworkers—the very people who were hardest hit by the Depression. As part of the package, the plan created the Agricultural Adjustment Administration. This organization paid farmers to reduce food production; farmers were actually given money not to grow or harvest crops like corn, rice, milk, wheat, and hogs. The goal was to raise prices, which had fallen during the 1920s, by making the products scarcer. Unfortunately, fewer crops meant less need for workers at a time when unemployment in the United States was more than 25 percent. Moreover, as people went hungry, milk was wasted and fruit rotted in the fields.

nomadic: moving from place to place with no permanent home.

Mexican Farmworkers

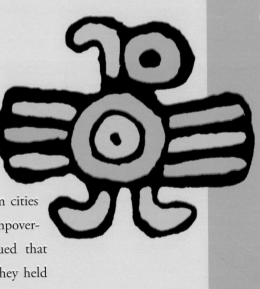

Steinbeck's work focused on the plight of white American farmers, but migrants also came from cities and towns, trading the destitution of city life for the impoverishment of the fields. Furthermore, Steinbeck argued that migrants of European descent were unique because they held land before becoming migrants. Steinbeck insisted that farmworkers of Mexican descent were a class of *nomadic* landless laborers. In fact, many Latinos owned land in the American Southwest before the Great Depression.

Well before the Mexican-American War of 1846–1848, Hispanic landowners cultivated the land that would one day become part of America. In 1835, the year that Mexico asserted

The First Hispanic Senator

n 1935 Dennis Chávez became the first Hispanic member of the United States Senate. Born in New Mexico in 1888, Chávez held his Senate seat for almost thirty years, until his death in 1962. His family traced their roots in New Mexico to a land grant given by the king of Spain in 1769. The senator's work included causes important to Hispanics, focusing particular effort on dealing with Puerto Rico's poverty during the 1940s.

its independence, the territory of Texas declared itself separate from Mexico. For the next ten years, over Mexico's objections, Texas regarded itself as independent. In 1845, the United States *annexed* Texas, and Mexico objected again. War resulted, culminating in an American march on Mexico City and Mexican defeat. The United States then seized the land that presently makes up Texas, California, Arizona, New Mexico, Colorado, Utah, and Nevada. Native Americans, Mexicans, and some white settlers all inhabited the region. Therefore, many of the Latino settlers who farmed the American Southwest did not come to the United States. The United States came to them.

In addition to those Latinos who already farmed the Southwest when it was taken over by the United States, others continued to migrate from the South. While stories of Eastern Americans settling in the American West are well known, few people realize that many of the West's settlers actually arrived from Mexico. Many were poor peasants who

Migrant workers' housing

worked hard and eventually earned enough money to buy a plot of farmland.

In Steinbeck's vision of the Great Depression, white farmers are forced from their land onto the migrant trail. When the Great Depression hit, however, Latino landowners also lost their land to creditors and joined in the migration westward to California. Latino migrant farmworkers often faced additional challenges on the migrant trail.

annexed: took over the territory.

adhered: followed a rule or agreement exactly.

Prejudice and Discrimination

n the 1930s, Latinos in California encountered discrimination. Like the Deep South, parts of California *adhered*

Woody Guthrie

oody Guthrie, a folk singer, songwriter, and migrant from the Dustbowl, captured the New Deal's effects in the opening verse to his song "Plane Wreck at Los Gatos":

The crops are all in and the peaches are rott'ning,
The oranges piled in their creosote dumps;
They're flying 'em back to the Mexican border
To pay all their money to wade back again

Another of Guthrie's songs captured the phenomenon of vigilante groups. Vigilantes are people who try to enforce the law as they see it without proper legal authority. During the Depression, vigilante groups patrolled farms and labor camps, keeping workers from effectively demanding better wages and working conditions. Guthrie's song "Vigilante Man" told of the brutality and injustice wrought by these often-violent people.

to segregationist policies. Segregation meant that access to parks, restaurants, movie theaters, and other public places was limited based on a person's skin color. Mexicans and Mexican Americans felt this discrimination acutely. California's *miscegenation* laws prevented people of different races from marrying. During the Depression, the U.S. government also deported many Mexican Americans. Some of those deported were actually American citizens. All this created an atmosphere mired in prejudice.

miscegenation: intermarriage, cohabitation, or sexual relations (leading to the birth of a child) between people of different races; an offensive term.

consolidated: combined into a single mass.

The Rise of Corporate Farms, the Bracero Program, and Social Unrest

Migrant workers in a canning factory

s small-scale farmers lost their lands, larger growers snapped up the farms and *consolidated* huge tracts of land. As a result, landowners became fewer and more powerful. Workers were hired by the growers, often for only a day, without a long-term contract or any direct link to the companies whose fruit and vegetables they picked and packed. These practices continue today.

In the 1930s, '40s, and '50s, migrant farmworkers' attempts to improve their situation were often brought to a swift and sometimes violent end. In Pixley, California, in 1933, for example, a farmers' vigilante group shot and killed two striking Mexican farmworkers as they attended a union meeting. Despite such oppression, strikes became common in the 1930s.

First Mexican American State Senator

Among those who worked hardest to bring an end to the Bracero Program was Henry Barbosa Gonzales. Born in Texas in 1916, Gonzales earned a bachelor's degree and a law degree before becoming the first Mexican American elected to the Texas Senate in 1961.

repatriation: to send someone back to his or her country of birth or from which he or she arrived.

pervaded: spread throughout something.

incendiary: causing civil unrest.

(A strike is an organized refusal to work until a grievance, like demands for better wages or working conditions, is met.)

As the 1930s drew to a close, World War II and an end to dry weather across the central United States drew the country out of its long economic stagnation. When the United States eventually joined the war late in 1941, many Americans went overseas to serve in the country's armed forces. Suddenly, American agriculture went from having far too many workers to having too few.

In response to labor demand, the deportation of Mexican Americans stopped. In fact, the policy of *repatriation* was reversed, and American farms actually began importing workers from Mexico. More than four million Mexican farmworkers

Farmworkers from Puerto Rico were flown to the mainland on military planes with no seating except lawn chairs.

came to work American fields from 1942 until 1964. The effort to import workers was known as the Bracero Program. (Bracero is a Spanish word that means "strong armed one.")

Wartime tensions and an influx of migrant labor led to social unrest. A year after the Bracero Program began, small clashes erupted between Mexican youths and white American military personnel in the Los Angeles area. While Latinos served in the American armed forces, racism *pervaded* popular culture. Fueled by *incendiary* newspaper accounts that inflamed the passions of restless military personnel, riots against Mexican Americans exploded across the city. Thousands of white military personnel and civilians took to the streets and attacked any Mexican American they could find. Eyewitness accounts, like those of Al Waxman cited by Cary McWilliams in *The Zoot Suit Riots,* tell of Los Angeles police officers descending into the violence to mete out vicious beatings of their own on Mexican Americans. (The clashes became known as the Zoot Suit Riots after the baggy style of dress young Mexican American men wore.)

The Bracero Program was meant to be temporary. Pressure from growers, especially

Latino farmworkers being recruited by the American government

those in California, convinced the government to extend the program, and it continued well beyond the war years. At the Bracero Program's peak in 1957, an estimated 192,000 braceros came to work on Californian farms, while another 150,000 were imported to work agricultural lands in other parts of the country. In fact, by 1960, 25 percent of all seasonal agricultural laborers were temporary braceros.

Growers had an amazing amount of control over the labor supply with the Bracero Program. When workers were needed, growers simply turned the right levers, and people flowed into the country. Just as easily, growers could reduce the supply. Yet with this flexibility came serious drawbacks. Farmworkers could be quickly deported; sometimes this included citizens. Low wages meant workers never escaped poverty. Braceros weren't guaranteed the same rights as citizens. Working and living conditions remained harsh. In 1964, under mounting criticism that the program was just a legalized form of slavery, the American government officially ended the Bracero Program.

By the 1960s, a large-scale migration pattern between Mexico and the United States was well established, and it continues today. The working conditions that had been tolerated under the Bracero Program were also well established—but the foundations of the unfair system were about to be shaken. In the 1960s, farmworkers began organizing, demanding better wages, treatment, and minimum safety standards. In the next chapter, we will see how the imaginative leadership of César Chávez and many others helped unionize agricultural workers across the American Southwest. Their cause captured the imagination of millions of American consumers who also began demanding the fair treatment of migrant farmworkers.

Habla Español

año (ahn-yo): year

trabajo (trah-bah-ho): work

tierra (tee-air-ah): land

dinero (dee-nare-oh): money

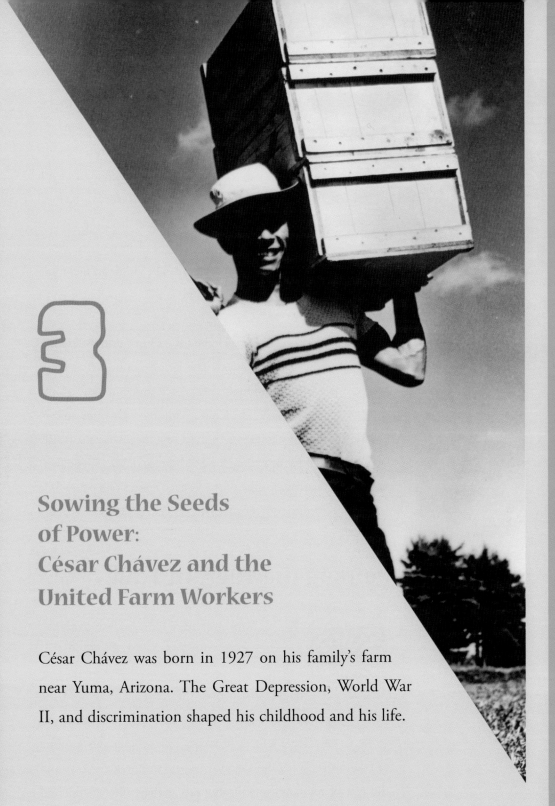

3

Sowing the Seeds of Power: César Chávez and the United Farm Workers

César Chávez was born in 1927 on his family's farm near Yuma, Arizona. The Great Depression, World War II, and discrimination shaped his childhood and his life.

Migrant workers' sleeping quarters

Chávez's grandfather came to the United States late in the nineteenth century. After several years working in Arizona's mines, he earned enough money to buy a farm near the Colorado River. The family prospered in the American desert. Their farm, fed by the Colorado River, produced enough wealth to make them comfortable. Chávez's father was elected the local postmaster and started three small businesses near the farm: a grocery store, a pool hall, and a garage. Farming, however, remained central to Chávez family life. The children, including César, learned to cultivate crops. The family seemed assured of security.

Then the Depression struck, and the three businesses failed. For a time, the farm remained. The family continued to cultivate crops and tend animals. Every day, migrants passed the farm on their way west. The Chávez children were often told to go and find hungry migrants in need of a meal, and the family became known for providing food to hungry travelers. The family at first was spared some of the Great Depression's pain while they helped reduce others' misery.

Joining the Migrant Trail

rought settled over the farm in 1933, and the family's fortunes shriveled. They fell into debt over taxes. In 1937, César's father joined the steady train of migrants heading to California. When he found work, he summoned César and the rest of his family in the hope that they, too, would find work in the fertile valleys of California. The family experienced all the hardships faced by other Latino migrant laborers. The

César Chávez

Migrant workers' housing

law offered them no safety or health protections. In 1936, the National Labor Relations Act took effect, but it excluded farmworkers from the protections given to other workers. Paid low wages, hired and fired at the whim of a grower, and desperate to keep starvation at bay, the entire family worked hard without ever making enough money to pay off their debt. Finally, in 1938, they lost their farm. They had become like millions of other Latino migrant laborers, traveling up and down California from harvest to harvest without a permanent home.

Constantly moving around, Chávez attended thirty-seven different schools, some segregated and some integrated. Education in California was English only, and teachers tried to stamp out Spanish among their pupils. Once, when César spoke Spanish, his teacher hung a sign around his neck that read "I am a clown, I speak Spanish." Discrimination like this was very different from anything Chávez had experienced in Arizona. After the eighth grade, Chávez dropped out of school to work full time in the fields. "It wasn't the learning I hated," Chávez said later, "but the conflicts." Despite his energy and intelligence, Chávez's eighth-grade education embarrassed him.

However, working full time in the fields taught him much more than the cultivation and harvest of nearly every crop in California. He also saw labor contractors and landowners cheating poor migrant farmworkers out of their earnings. Chávez's father refused to work on farms being struck by workers unhappy with their wages or treatment. Early developments of an agricultural workers' movement had begun to form, including attempts at creating small unions. Chávez's father joined some of these, and occasionally the groups won victories against growers and contractors.

A Life of Nonviolent Action

n 1944, Chávez left farmwork and joined the U.S. Navy. He served two years, returning in 1946 to work in the fields. In 1948, he married Helen Fabela. Together, they helped Latino farmworkers learn to read and write. Around this time, Chávez's interest in nonviolent political leaders took hold, and he poured over the biographies of people like Mahatma Gandhi and St. Francis of Assisi. Not until 1952, however, after meeting John Ross, did Chávez begin considering a leadership role in the farmworker community.

John Ross had been employed under Roosevelt's New Deal as a worker at a migrant labor camp in California, and by the 1950s, he was involved with the Community Service Organization (CSO). The CSO worked to ensure Latino civil rights and combat discrimination and police brutality. It registered Latino voters and played a role in the desegregation of schools, theaters, and other public spaces in southern California. In addition, the group was instrumental in getting several police officers punished for the savage beating of a group of Mexican Americans in 1951.

Initially skeptical of what he heard, Chávez slowly warmed to Ross. Chávez eventually agreed to work for the CSO registering Latinos to vote and giving citizenship classes to Latino farmworkers. He threw himself into the cause with amazing energy, tirelessly putting in a day's work in the fields and then spending all evening going door-to-door signing up voters.

The CSO voter registration drive increased Latino voters in California by tens of thousands. For the next decade, Chávez's efforts helped foster twenty-two CSO chapters across the state. The group helped combat discrimination against Latinos and get better *infrastructure* and sanitation into the migrant *barrios*. In 1959, Chávez was made the CSO's executive director.

By 1962, Chávez had come to believe the best way to improve Latino farmworkers' situation was through a full-fledged labor movement. From 1962 until 1965, Chávez, along with his wife Helen Chávez and Dolores Huerta, a single mother and teacher who worked with the CSO, built a union from scratch.

Blacklists, Boycotts, and the Birth of the United Farm Workers

ésar Chávez, Helen Chávez, and Dolores Huerta agreed that, at first, it was important not to call the movement a union. Both growers and workers feared what a union might bring. Growers wanted to avoid strikes in the fields, while workers knew that very often, a strike led only

Dolores Huerta

olores Huerta's work with farmworkers began when, as a teacher, she saw the poverty the children of agricultural workers endured. She later said, "I couldn't stand seeing kids come to class hungry and needing shoes. I thought I could do more by organizing farmworkers than by trying to teach their hungry children." Her organizing efforts began in the San Joaquin Valley, a major fruit-growing region of California, where she encouraged many workers to sign up for the quickly forming union. As the movement gained strength, she became an indispensable negotiator, demanding higher wages and better working conditions for farmworkers.

to short-term gains in wages and working conditions. In the longer term, workers who struck were *blacklisted*, fired, or even beaten up. The name chosen for the group was therefore a cautious one: the National Farm Workers Association (NFWA).

When the Chávezes and Huerta began their movement, workers had no minimum wage and were often paid so poorly that keeping a family out of poverty, even if children worked, was virtually impossible. Farmworkers were not eligible for unemployment insurance and had no guarantee of *Social Security*, something most workers had come to

President Roosevelt

expect since President Roosevelt introduced it as part of his New Deal. Moreover, workers who complained were easily replaced. Although the last temporary foreign agricultural workers came to the United States in 1963 under the Bracero Program, growers pressured the federal administration in Washington to allow braceros back into the country. Despite the large population of agricultural workers available for employment, growers convinced the government that labor shortages loomed on the horizon.

Braceros were allowed back into the United States in 1965, but the government insisted they be paid at least $1.40 an hour. American workers, however, typically earned between $1.00 and $1.25, and growers were under no obligation to raise these wages. Despite the government's minimum wage requirement, many growers paid the braceros less than $1.40 per hour. Very often, braceros were preferred because they were more easily intimidated into remaining silent about working conditions and wages that kept them destitute. For example, in 1957, over one-third of the labor camps in the San Joaquin Valley were considered to be unfit for human habitation. If braceros complained or unionized, a grower could easily have them deported.

The differences between the wages paid to U.S.-born workers and those paid to for-

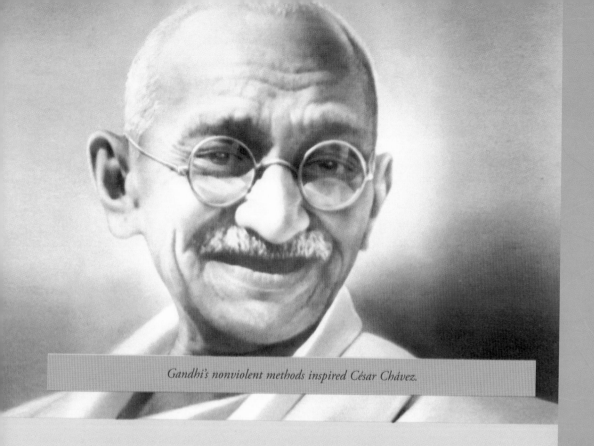

Gandhi's nonviolent methods inspired César Chávez.

eign-born braceros led to problems. In 1965, when Filipino farmworkers struck the Delano, California, grape growers, the mostly Mexican American NFWA, led by Chávez and Huerta, joined in. They wanted growers to match the wages paid to domestic workers with those of imported workers.

fallow: unseeded.

Strikes plowed through the fertile soil of labor discontent, following the crop harvests northward all summer. To cries of "*¡Huelga!*" (a word that means both "strike" and "let *fallow*"), work stopped and laborers took up picket signs demanding things like a twenty-cent raise.

Law-enforcement officials were hesitant to stop angry growers from intimidating workers, and sometimes violence was used on picketers. César Chávez insisted that workers not respond with violence of their own. His models for resistance were inspired by the nonviolent examples of people like Gandhi, but sometimes violence flared on both sides.

43

Grapes ready for harvest

Farmworkers' button

As the harvest season turned to late fall and winter, the grapes remained on the vines, unpicked and rotting. The town of Delano became well known to the nation. The California State Senate Factfinding Subcommittee on Un-American Activities arrived to investigate the strike. Senator Robert Kennedy, a Democratic senator from Massachusetts and brother to former President John F. Kennedy, sat on the panel alongside Senator George Murphy, a Republican from California who had close associations with the Californian agricultural industry. At one hearing, Chávez testified that the same protections workers in American factories, offices, and on construction crews were given should be available to farmworkers. He stated, "Ranchers in Delano say that the farmworkers are happy living the way they are—just like the southern plantation owner used to say about the Negroes."

The NFWA's first major effort to bring attention to the plight of farmworkers occurred in 1966. Beginning in San Francisco, the union began a 340-mile march that would end in Sacramento, California's state capital. Known as the Peregrinacion, or Pilgrimage, the marchers walked an average of fifteen miles a day through the countryside. It was a painful journey. Marchers developed blisters from walking, and some had blood seep through their shoes. As the march continued, supporters rallied around the farmworkers. Along the route, strangers eagerly opened their doors, offering meals and beds to sleep on. "Our pilgrimage is the match," one farmworker said, "that will light our cause for all farmworkers to see what is happening here." As a result of the attention, one of California's largest vineyards, the primary target of the strike, which had begun in 1965, agreed to the first union contract between a grower and a farmworkers' union.

Later in the year, the National Farm Workers Association

Walnut Growers!

WHY share walnut returns with an independent packer?

WHY not keep his profit for yourself?

JOIN the 25 year old, non-profit cooperative association that handles 85% of the entire state crop.

112 new members have signed up already this year. There's a reason!

Apply, while membership is open, to any local walnut association, or to

Calfornia Walnut Growers Association

1745 East 7th St., Los Angeles

An advertisement for organizing walnut pickers

Your appreciation of the California Cultivator can be shown best by writing to and buying from Cultivator advertisers.

merged with the Agricultural Workers Organizing Committee, the Filipino-dominated group that had begun the grape strike in 1965. Chávez became the director of the newly created United Farm Workers Organizing Committee, which later became known simply as the United Farm Workers (UFW). The group won concessions from major corporations, including the biggest company in California, DiGiogio. Yet many other growers did not want to give in to the union. Workers were brought in illegally from Mexico to replace those on strike.

Chávez's adherence to nonviolent struggle led him to find imaginative ways of furthering union goals. When tempers ran high among the executives of the newly formed

Strawberry pickers

union, Chávez announced that he would fast until each and every union organizer renewed their pledge to nonviolence. Although bursts of violence sometimes accompanied union efforts to achieve better wages, Chávez's effort worked remarkably well. In fact, in 1974, César Chávez received the Martin Luther King Nonviolent Peace Award from Coretta Scott King, the Reverend Martin Luther King's widow.

The most famous, and effective, nonviolent tactic Chávez used was boycotts. In one example, people across North America stopped consuming California table grapes. Farmworkers were sent to New York, Ohio, and Pittsburgh, Pennsylvania, in the East, and Montreal and Toronto in Canada to drum up support for their efforts in California. By 1970, the action paid off, and growers from major corporate ranches eventually signed deals with the union. The success was short-lived, however; by 1973, the major growers refused to renew contracts and attempted to undermine the farmworkers union. Chávez renewed the grape boycott. From 1973 to 1975, an estimated seventeen million Americans took part in boycotting grapes.

Students, religious leaders, and ordinary citizens flocked to the movement's ideals. Public officials took notice, and pressure mounted from grape companies who wanted an end to boycotts and the negative publicity campaigns. In 1975, pressure from growers prompted Governor Edmund G. "Jerry" Brown to pass a law protecting farmworkers. The Agricultural Labor Relations Act guaranteed workers the right to organize and bargain with employers.

Strikes against growers of various crops rolled across California, Arizona, and Texas during the 1970s. Workers continued to sign contracts with large corporations. By 1980, UFW membership had swollen to an estimated 100,000 workers. Divisions in the union, however, weakened it. Some workers complained that the UFW executive positions were being filled by the college educated and no longer reflected its roots among ordinary farmworkers. The complaints came to a head, resulting in the dismissal of seven workers who had stood for election against the union-selected candidates for local representation. Chávez was criticized for his heavy-handed tactics, and the union lost a lawsuit brought

pro-agribusiness: in favor of farming as an industry.

amnesty: a pardon from the usual punishment given for having performed an illegal act.

by the seven fired farmworkers for wrongful dismissal from their jobs.

With the union divided, farmers found it easier to challenge. One result was that fewer workers were hired by farmers directly. Instead, labor contractors began to act as middlemen, hiring workers and then contracting out their work crews to growers. By contracting out employment to contractors, growers could skirt the burdens union contracts put on them. They no longer had to hire UFW members and instead simply hired contractors. Undocumented Mexican laborers were recruited by some contractors, a trend that continues today. Union membership declined as Mexican-born migrants supplanted American-born migrant workers.

Ronald Reagan had been the *pro-agribusiness* governor of California during the tumultuous years of early union organizing. In 1986, as President of the United States, Ronald Reagan granted the new braceros *amnesty* from immigration enforcement. On the positive side, this brought around three million undocumented farmworkers out from under the shroud that kept them from the protection of the law. Today, many of these people and their children provide a valuable contribution to the country. On the other side, Reagan's action gave an encouraging signal to other migrants who were considering entering the United States illegally. As a result, a new farm labor surplus occurred across the United States as waves of immigrants crossed the border in the hopes that they would be granted legal-resident status as well. This further drove down the wages of the farmworkers hired by contractors and diminished the strength of the union.

Chávez continued his fight for farmworker rights throughout the 1980s and into the 1990s. Pesticide use became a new focus for him. Pesticides are poisonous chemicals used to control insects and other pests that destroy farm crops. His "Wrath of Grapes" campaign helped bring pesticide poisoning of agricultural workers to the conscience of North America.

Immigration also became a focus of concern for the UFW in the 1990s and remains one to this day. The union does not believe that the presence of unauthorized workers depresses wages. Rather it is unauthorized workers' fear of joining unions that discourages wages from rising. Many in the union understand that those who are coming to the United States in search of work do so to have a better life for themselves and their families.

When Chávez died in 1993, forty thousand mourners followed his plain pine casket on a final pilgrimage to Delano. By the time of his death, the union was clearly less powerful than it had once been. Its membership had shrunk to twenty thousand by 1994, although it rebounded to twenty-seven thousand by the year 2000. Some of the union's gains eroded in the 1980s when California began to loosen enforcement of the laws protecting farmworkers. Negotiating a union contract with a corporation only to have the corporation restructure is risky business that reduces the number of workers that fall under the terms of the agreement reached. Reaching agreements with companies that hire most workers during peak seasons continues to prove difficult.

"Regardless of what the future holds for our union," Chávez once said, "regardless of what the future holds for farmworkers, our accomplishments cannot be undone. The consciousness and the pride that were raised by our union are alive and thriving inside millions of young Hispanics who will never work on a farm."

The Struggle Continues Today

hile many Latinos live in American cities and many occupy the country's middle class, to this day, hundreds of thousands of other Latinos still work on American farms. Approximately seventeen of every twenty farmworkers speak Spanish. Moreover, young Latino migrants—the average age of a farmworker is thirty-one—

Ronald Reagan

onald Wilson Reagan was born in Tampico, Illinois, on February 6, 1911. Before becoming President of the United States, Reagan spent two decades working as an actor in Hollywood. He became president of the Screen Actors Guild—and then, in 1966, he became Governor of California and was reelected in 1970. His success in politics continued, and he won the 1980 Republican presidential nomination. In 1981, after being elected President, Reagan was shot in an attempted assassination. He recovered and went on to lead a successful presidency, winning reelection in 1984. His death in 2004 after a long battle with Alzheimer's disease led to an outpouring of grief and respect throughout the world, with former British Prime Minister Margaret Thatcher, former Canadian Prime Minister Brian Mulroney, and former leader of the Soviet Union Mikhail Gorbachev attending his funeral.

continue to spill over the border in the hopes of making a life for themselves on American farms. The National Agricultural Workers Survey reports that over eight out of every ten farmworkers come from another country.

Today, whether foreign-born farmworkers come from Mexico or from countries further south, those attempting to cross the U.S. border illegally are increasingly funneled through remote desert border crossings. Their experience often brings them into contact with people smugglers (known as coyotes), *la migra* (the slang term given to the immigration officials patrolling the border), or worse—vigilantes who lawlessly prowl the seemingly endless expanse of the American Southwest. Once in the United States, migrant farmworkers confront the problems of safety, living, and working conditions. But the dangerous challenges they face started much sooner—the moment they undertook their journey to cross the border. In the next chapter, we look at the experience of migrant farmworkers who must cross international borders to find work.

Habla Español

dirección (dee-rake-see-own): direction, leadership

dignidad (deeg-nee-dahd): dignity

fruta (froo-tah): fruit

uva (oo-vah): grape

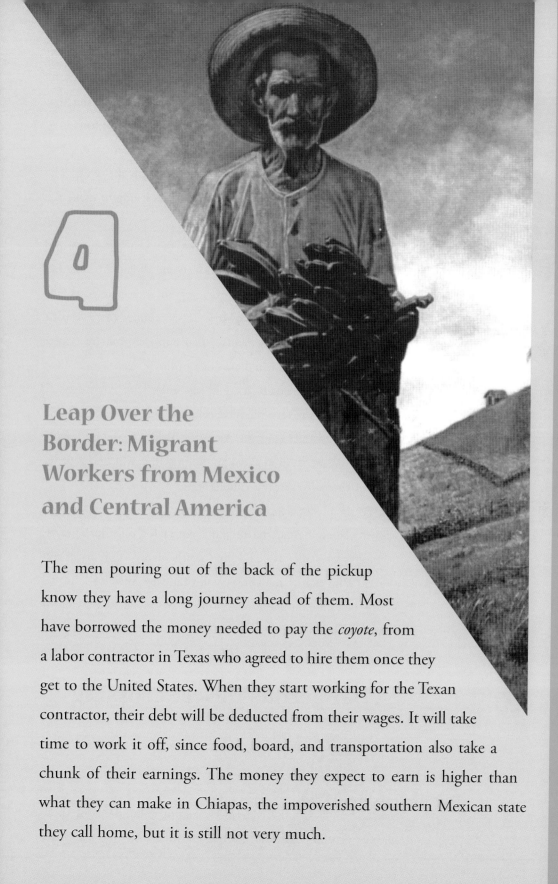

Leap Over the Border: Migrant Workers from Mexico and Central America

The men pouring out of the back of the pickup know they have a long journey ahead of them. Most have borrowed the money needed to pay the *coyote*, from a labor contractor in Texas who agreed to hire them once they get to the United States. When they start working for the Texan contractor, their debt will be deducted from their wages. It will take time to work it off, since food, board, and transportation also take a chunk of their earnings. The money they expect to earn is higher than what they can make in Chiapas, the impoverished southern Mexican state they call home, but it is still not very much.

A sign along the U.S.-Mexican border warns immigrants of extreme temperatures.

Already the temperature is falling as the sun makes its descent over the horizon. Their coyote is busy checking that everyone has full water containers. The desert is unforgiving, one of the harshest climates on Earth, with searing daytime temperatures and little rainfall for most of the year. The migrants know that one traveler a day dies trying to make the crossing.

There is hushed talk of *la migra*, the U.S. Customs and Border Patrol, but the coyote also fears the vigilante bands that have begun patrolling the border region in recent years. He knows that making it through the desert requires that everyone follows his instructions. Worse than apprehension by border agents, any mistakes could cost one of the migrants more than the up-front fee he paid. It could cost a life.

When the sun sets, the travelers grow anxious. Some already have family working in the American fields. Some are leaving behind children. All of them are hoping they will find a better life for themselves in the United States.

As the pickup speeds off, heading south toward the Mexican town of Santa Ana, the migrants kneel for one final prayer. Minutes later, they rise and slip into the dense scrub brush and cacti. With hardly the whisper of a footstep, they settle into a pace, one migrant ahead of another in single file, and disappear into the dusk.

A Dangerous Desert Crossing

t the Mexico-U.S. border, hundreds of thousands of unreported border crossings like this one take place

The land along the border is often barren and rugged.

Graffiti decorates the wall along the U.S.-Mexican border.

every year under the cover of darkness. Nighttime helps shield migrants from the watchful gaze of border guards who patrol the frontier with the aim of stopping the flow of the approximately one million undocumented Mexicans and Central Americans attempting to enter the United States each year. Nighttime also protects migrants from sunstroke and heat exhaustion caused by the blazing desert sun. Temperatures in the remote regions of the Arizona desert, today one of the busiest border-crossings in North America, can reach higher than 115° F (46° C).

Increasingly, illegal border crossings are moving away from the more populated areas of the Mexico-U.S. border into the Southwest's remote regions. In response to the terrorist attacks of September 11, 2001, the United States has beefed up security along its southern border. Fences, video surveillance, infrared cameras, and air patrols are some of the ways American authorities have tried to combat migrant entry into the United States. Recent American border operations include

The border

Operation Hold the Line in El Paso (1993), Operation Gatekeeper in San Diego (1994), Operation Safeguard in Tucson (1995), and Operation Rio Grande in the South Rio Grande Valley of Texas (1997). The measures have pushed migrants deeper into the desert, where there are no fences and fewer surveillance measures.

At least 139 migrants died trying to walk through the desert in 2003. For the entire Mexico-U.S. border, the approximate death toll is around one person a day. It is likely, however, that many other people lie dead on the desert floor uncounted. The numbers are higher than they were in the past. In May of 2003, nineteen migrants died after being sealed in a sweltering container truck and driven across the border by a driver paid $7500 to smuggle the people into the United States. Car chases between migrants and border guards have resulted in fatal accidents.

The danger of a desert crossing has prompted many migrants to rely on the services of the coyotes, the people smugglers and indispensable desert guides. Coyotes know the terrain. They know the watering holes, guiding landmarks, and the safe houses on the other side of the inhospitable expanse. They also know how to avoid border guards, directing migrants to sleep during the day if they can, and erasing their footprints left in the dirt,

unscrupulous: without
moral principles.

the tell-tale trail of a crossing, which risks alerting the border patrol to their illegal presence. Without the coyotes, successful passage through the desert would be nearly impossible. In places, the landscape is thick with cacti and populated with poisonous animals like rattlesnakes and scorpions. The parched region offers a scant water supply. Travelers are careful not to waste the supplies they carry with them. When they do find water, they collect it, replenishing their bottles before their thirst causes them to drain the containers.

But coyotes charge a high price for their services. The going rate to be transported through such an inhospitable climate is around $2,000 per person. Many Mexicans and migrants from other Latin American countries cannot afford to pay the fees up front and are forced into debt even before they enter the United States. There is no refund if they are stopped by the border guards and sent home. Their choice is to either remain in their home country, slowly paying off the debt, or try again to enter the United States, incurring further debt in the process. In fact, according to *Migrant News*, a publication produced by the University of California at Davis, about half of the Mexican migrants apprehended along the border had been caught earlier in the same year while attempting a crossing.

Migrants get money to pay coyotes from friends and relatives. It is also common, however, to have labor contractors lend money on the condition that the migrant work for the contractor until the debt is paid. If a migrant is lucky, he can work the money off over the course of a harvest season. Rebelling against an *unscrupulous* labor contractor can lead to threats of violence against the migrant or the migrant's family.

Caught!

igrant News reports that at the busy Arizona border, 400,000 migrants are caught trying to enter the United States illegally every year. This means that one in every four attempts to enter the United States ends with American authorities capturing the migrants in Arizona. Most are photographed and fingerprinted, and then returned to Mexico. Only three thousand criminal prosecutions take place. In total, the number of undocumented migrants who cross into the United States each year declined after September 11, 2001. In 2000, 1.6 million people made the journey. The number was only 900,000 in 2003.

Once across the border, migrants come into contact with all sorts of other people. They are put up in a safe house, usually for one night but sometimes for three or four. They are then given a ride to what will become their American home base, most commonly located in California, Texas, or Florida. From these bases, they join the estimated one to three million other migrant laborers on the American harvest trail.

Vigilantes Taking the Law into Their Own Hands

he influx of migrant workers has led to a backlash among some sections of the American population who feel increasing numbers of foreign-born Latinos are destabilizing the country. Inspired at least in part by what they perceive as government mishandling of the border in the post–September 11 world, some people have taken to patrolling remote points along the Mexico-U.S. border, attempting to stem the flow of migrants. Many are members of *militia* groups. They count former military personnel, former police officers, former immigration officials, and ranchers among their members. Some also have ties to racist organizations advocating *white supremacy*. Many people believe that the actions of vigilante groups along the border are motivated more by anti-Mexican feelings and fears of foreigners than a genuine belief that the vigilantes are helping American security. Yet vigilante groups, or citizen militias as they prefer to be called, maintain that they are performing a service for the country by taking the law into their own hands.

Gross Domestic Product

country's wealth is calculated using per capita Gross Domestic Product (GDP)—the total number of goods and services produced by a country divided by the country's population. Countries are ranked by this measurement of wealth. Since per capita GDP is only an average, some people fall above and some fall below the figure given. Per capita GDP also does not take into account the differences between regions. For example, Mexico's northern area has become increasingly wealthy in recent years, but its southern area remains relatively poor. The per capita GDP of Mexico, however, shows how much money people would have if the country's wealth were evenly distributed over all regions and therefore does not give a completely accurate picture of what real people's lives are like. Despite its shortcomings, per capita GDP is considered a reliable indicator of a country's wealth. Below are the GDPs and rankings of some selected countries.

Luxembourg: $55,100 – 1st

United States: $37,800 – 2nd

Canada: $29,700 – 12th

Mexico: $9,000 – 85th

World Average: $8,200

El Salvador: $4,800 – 128th

Guatemala : $4,100 – 135th

In places, the border is marked only by a chain-link fence.

Vigilantes have no legal power, no formal training unless previously employed by immigration or another government agency, and routinely violate the rights of migrants who, although in the country illegally, are still guaranteed many of the civil and political rights enjoyed by everyone in the United States. Vigilantes violate migrants' human rights, and activists argue that the United States must do more to protect the human dignity and integrity of migrants. Reports state that gun-carrying groups have robbed migrants and have used excessive physical force, including detaining people at gunpoint. Most experts agree that it is only a matter of time before a violent tragedy takes place in the border region of the Southwest. Currently, the Department of Justice says it is investigating the issue.

Despite the dangers, many undocumented migrants are willing to cross the border to escape poverty. The wages of the average farmworker might seem low to Americans working in other industries; the $7,500 annual wage is certainly much lower than what most people in the United States need to survive. But the money compares favorably to the wages paid in the poorest regions of Mexico, where levels of wealth are similar to neighboring Guatemala. The gross domestic product per person in Guatemala is $4,100. Seventy-five percent of the population lives below the poverty line, and around half of the country's citizens work as poor rural farmers.

Finding enough money left over to provide for themselves and their families can be difficult for the migrants. The money it costs to come to the United States often forces migrant workers into debt, and living expenses add up. If they can save money to send home, however, it goes much further in their home countries because the American dollar is worth more after it is exchanged into local currency. Therefore, despite the challenges, many people are willing to make great sacrifices to seek employment as America's harvesters.

Increasing Understanding and Legalizing Migration

exan and Arizonan *nativists* might fear the rising Latino population within the borders of their own states, but most Americans are open to the Latino population. According to the most recent U.S. census data from 2003, 39.9 million Latinos call the United States home, approximately 13.7 percent of the total American population. This is up from 2000, when there were about 35.3 million Latinos making up 12.5

nativists: those who believe that native inhabitants should receive favored treatment.

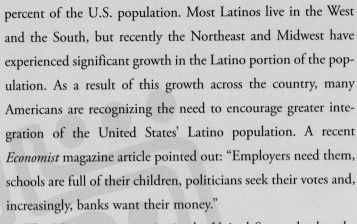

consular: pertaining to the government official working in a foreign country.

percent of the U.S. population. Most Latinos live in the West and the South, but recently the Northeast and Midwest have experienced significant growth in the Latino portion of the population. As a result of this growth across the country, many Americans are recognizing the need to encourage greater integration of the United States' Latino population. A recent *Economist* magazine article pointed out: "Employers need them, schools are full of their children, politicians seek their votes and, increasingly, banks want their money."

The Mexican community in the United States also has the support of the Mexican government. Vincente Fox, Mexico's President, has been pushing to bring illegal Mexican workers out of the shadows through the creation of a temporary worker program, possibly similar to the Bracero Program of previous generations. However, alongside these efforts, the Mexican government is also advocating the legalization of many undocumented migrants. The efforts are an attempt to address an issue that has long remained unresolved in North America. Even with a continent-wide free trade agreement (NAFTA) between Canada, the United States, and Mexico, which allows for the free flow of goods across borders, nothing allows for the free flow of labor.

Attempting to address the issue, President Fox created the Institute for Mexicans Abroad, which has offices at Mexican *consular* offices in the United States. The aim of the project is to educate Mexican migrant workers about their rights and give them information about healthcare and financial resources. Furthermore, the program has established the *matricula consular*, which, as the *Economist* notes, is accepted as a valid identification document by more than eight hundred lawenforcement agencies across the United States. So far, over 1.5 million cards have been granted. This has helped to bring many illegal

Potato pickers

Latino immigrants plan for financial future for both themselves and their families.

Mexican migrants into the open, giving them access to services that previous generations of undocumented workers never enjoyed.

Mexicans living in the United States are as important to Mexico as they are to the United States. In 2003, Mexicans living in the United States sent well over $14 billion to their families. This money is known as remittances. Only oil exports were a bigger source of that country's income. Across the border, in the United States, businesses are eager for a share of the money. U.S. banks have begun to accept nontraditional forms of I.D., like the *matricula consular,* from people wishing to open bank accounts. Many of those banks—eighty-six out of 118—are based in the Midwest. The hope is to gain long-term

Chances are, these apples were picked by migrant workers.

business from migrant workers. When migrants stay in the United States, many eventually require mortgages to buy homes, educational savings programs for American-born children, and checking accounts. American businesses want to take a part in this often-neglected sector of the economy.

The recognition of the importance and contribution of foreign-born migrant farm-workers to the United States exposes the contradiction between the country's immigration-control policies and its need for low-cost labor. At a time when border enforcement is being strengthened, labor-law enforcement is being weakened. The result is a declining standard of living for migrants and a cheapening of their wages. The agricultural industry benefits enormously from the low-skilled, low-wage labor coming into America from across its southern border. Yet, once foreign-born migrants arrive, the conditions they face are often anything but welcoming. Undocumented workers live in continual fear of *la migra* even after entering the United States.

Once embarking on the American harvest trail, migrants, both foreign-born and citizens alike, share many of the same challenges. The housing conditions in labor camps are often dismal. It is often overcrowded and unsanitary. Widespread poverty is another related problem. The children of migrants often suffer from poor educational experiences as they move through many schools while migrating from state to state, which can lead to a vicious cycle of impoverishment across generations. Exposure to pesticides, workplace hazards, and in some extreme cases the total lack of hygiene facilities also contribute to serious health issues among migrant agricultural workers. Their poor wages leave many workers unable to afford medical treatment in all but the most serious of injuries and health problems.

The result of these living and working conditions is the lowest standard of living among any employed group in the United States. Migrant farmworkers, whether in the country legally or illegally, are not even guaranteed the minimum wage or minimum safety standards enjoyed by nearly every other legal worker in the country, and for these reasons they suffer enormously. In the next chapter we take an in-depth look at what real life is like on the harvest trail and how migrant farmworkers and their families struggle every day.

Habla Español

frontera (frone-tare-ah): border

trabajador (trah-bah-hah-door): worker

salud (sah-lewd): health

día (dee-ah): day

5

Life on the Harvest Trail

Life on the harvest trail is difficult. Whether migrants are based in Florida, Texas, or California, living a nomadic life in the United States poses common hardships. With poor wages, poor housing, and poor sanitary conditions, migrant farmworkers occupy the lowest rung on the American economic ladder.

Strawberries are just one of the many crops picked by migrant workers.

Legislation that aims to improve the opportunities available to migrant workers currently exists. The Migrant and Seasonal Agricultural Worker Protection Act attempts to regulate labor contractors and reduce the amount of economic exploitation workers face. The law requires that workers be told how much they will earn and then be paid that amount. They must be informed about hours, working conditions, and housing if it is provided. Furthermore, workers are supposed to be informed of deductions to their wages and what these deductions are for.

Laws like this offer some protection, but unscrupulous labor contractors sometimes take advantage of labor and educational barriers that farmworkers face. For example, some labor contractors directly disobey the law by reducing wages through *fictitious* deductions. Even deductions that look legitimate can be fictitious. For instance, some farmworkers who don't have Social Security numbers still have Social Security deducted from their paychecks, even though without a Social Security number no deductions can legally be made by the government. In such cases, the labor contractors are usually deducting the money and pocketing it. Actions like these can get a contractor into trouble with the law, but conditions like poverty, lack of education, or illegal work status make farmworkers feel they are unable to report abuses.

fictitious: false; fake.

Imagine for a moment that you are a migrant farmworker and you suspect money is being unfairly skimmed from your paycheck. What will you do? With your low wages, you cannot afford to hire a lawyer. Even if you can seek help, what will the result be? What will stop your employer from firing you the moment he hears that you are "causing trouble"? What will happen to your family if you get fired? Worse yet, what if someone threatens you or your family to intimidate you into silence? Do you think you might be willing to simply put up with the injustice to ensure you still have a job and safety tomorrow? Many farmworkers make precisely this decision.

Adequate Housing: An Elusive Necessity

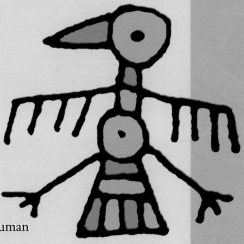

dequate housing is one of the most basic human needs, and yet it remains elusive to many migrant farmworkers. Migrants often try to save money by cramming numerous

scavenge: look through
discarded things for
something usable.

impels: forces.

people into a single unit and splitting the rent. The poorest migrants, often those trying to pay off their smuggling debts, live in overcrowded conditions. In Florida and California, for example, ten to twelve people routinely live in a one-bedroom trailer. Many of these migrants do not enjoy the luxury of a bed. Some sleep on the floor without a pillow or sheets. People may *scavenge* old blankets, cushions, or even cardboard to spread across the floor. If mattresses are available, they are likely shared among more than one worker. Pests like cockroaches, rats, and mice are common in the overcrowded and unclean conditions.

Steven Greenhouse of the *New York Times* reported in a 1998 article titled "As U.S. Economy Booms, Housing for Migrant Workers Worsens" that workers lived in garages, tool sheds, caves, fields, and parking lots where they suffered in unsanitary conditions. "In Orange County, N.Y., an hour from New York City, raw sewage formed puddles outside migrant worker's trailers," wrote Greenhouse. He added, "In Mecca, Calif., more than 100 migrants slept in parking lots along the road." Squatter camps, neighborhoods of lean-to housing made from scraps of plastic, cardboard, wood, and other materials, dot some agricultural counties recalling images of the most impoverished areas of the countries migrants left behind.

Today, according to the Housing Assistance Council in Washington, D.C., approximately 800,000 farmworkers lack adequate housing. The high number of workers in the United States from Mexico and Central American countries has created a surplus in labor. These workers are willing to accept poor living and working conditions because the wages they will earn, despite being the lowest paid to any group of American workers, are higher than what they would earn in their own country. The prospect of rescuing their families from poverty *impels* them to cut costs on things like housing, in the hope of saving as much money as possible.

The homes provided for farmworkers are substandard.

Migrant housing is often unsafe and dirty.

Today, labor contractors and growers must get specific authorization if they are going to provide housing and transportation services. Housing must meet federal housing standards. However, instead of improving the living conditions of migrant workers, the result has been the creation of a housing shortage. Rather than bring housing up to federal standards, labor contractors and growers have stopped providing housing at all. Individual housing providers have sprung up to meet the substantial housing demand, but they charge a high rent for poor housing.

Housing inspections must take place twice a year, but this requirement is not always enforced. With such low wages, migrants cannot afford to live in more expensive housing. While it seems that closing down unsafe and unsanitary housing is a step toward ensuring a better quality of life for farmworkers, measures like these also have negative consequences. If too many housing units are deemed unsuitable for habitation and closed down, then pressure mounts on the existing spaces available. Decreasing the housing supply increases the rent for the remaining units. The only choice left to the workers is to pay high rents for poor-quality shelter—or go homeless.

Dangers in the Workplace

chronic: long-lasting or recurring frequently.

neurological: pertaining to the nervous system.

overty also drives migrant farmworkers to tolerate workplace dangers that most Americans would reject. One of the most dangerous risk factors workers face is pesticides. In the United States, farmers use about 1.2 billion pounds (about 500 million kilograms) of pesticides annually. The pesticides used on American fields weigh the same as the total amount of grain consumed by China's 1.3 billion residents every year. Thinking about this in other terms, American pesiticide use totals approximately 4.13 pounds (1.87 kg) per American per year.

Pesticides don't just kill the insects in farmers' fields; they also seep into the food supply where they are eventually consumed by Americans, leading to health risks for everyone. The first people, however, to show signs of pesticide exposure are farmworkers. Every year, 300,000 farmworkers are directly exposed to pesticides and suffer pesticide-related illnesses and injuries. Skin rashes, irritated eyes, flu-like illnesses, nausea, and light-headedness are some of the early sicknesses that develop from this kind of chemical poisoning. In the long-term, *chronic* illnesses can develop, which reduce life expectancy and quality of life. Pesticides have been linked to birth defects, sterility, *neurological* damage, liver disease, and kidney disease. In counties with many farms, researchers have also found cancer clusters. (Cancer clusters are regions where unexpectedly high rates of cancer plague a local population.) In the case of regions where there are intensive farming operations, cancer clusters might indicate exposure to cancer-causing agents like pesticides.

"In the old days, miners would carry birds with them to warn against poison gas. Hopefully, the birds would die before the miners. Farmworkers are society's canaries."
—César Chávez

In the past, migrant farmworkers would sometimes find themselves drenched in poison from a passing crop duster, a low-flying aircraft that sprays fields with pesticides. They felt the cool chemicals land on their skin, and after a few seconds, the burning began. The poison mist in the air choked their breathing. Today, laws are in place to prevent people from working in fields while the fields are being sprayed. Even if the laws are respected, however, the risk of pesticide drift still exists when chemical vapors sprayed on neighboring fields are carried on the wind into a field where workers are harvesting.

Furthermore, not all changes to the laws governing pesticides result in improvements for workers. In 1996, the Environmental Protection Agency in fact weakened pesticide protection for workers. It is now legal to work in a field for up to five days without being informed of the risk of pesticides. Incidents of skin rashes, a telltale sign of chemical exposure, doubled between 1998 and 2001, with twenty-two of every thousand workers reporting a rash, up from the previous eleven of every thousand workers. Since most workers only seek medical attention for very serious injuries, it is likely pesticide-related injury is underreported. Furthermore, not all farmworkers are trained to recognize the signs of pesticide poisoning. In the Southeast, 46 percent of workers said they received no pesticide-related training, while in California, where workers have enjoyed legal protections for over three decades, 24 percent reported a lack of training.

When and if workers are informed of the risks of pesticides, they change their behavior to limit exposure. For example, farmworkers aware of the risks take off their shoes and strip off their outer layer of clothing before they enter their houses at the end of the day. These measures, as simple as they sound, help to improve a farmworker's chances of remaining in good health by leaving chemicals behind at the doorstep. Farmworkers will also take extra care to wash the chemicals from their skin at the end of the day. This, however, can only be done if running water and proper sanitation facilities are provided.

The first Occupational Safety and Health Act was put in place in 1970, but it was not until 1987 that guidelines were issued for sanitation facilities for farmworkers. As a result of the new laws, toilets are required, drinking water must be supplied, and handwashing facilities must be available to those who work in the field. Employers must also inform their workers about the importance of good hygiene. Good hygiene reduces the incidence of disease, including respiratory illnesses, eye disease, and urinary and intestinal tract infections—and it helps limit pesticide exposure. By providing handwashing facilities, farmworkers' lives are dramatically improved. The guidelines for sanitation facilities, however, do not apply in the states of California, Arizona, Oregon, Washington State, North Carolina, Virginia, Tennessee, New Mexico, Michigan, Hawaii, Maryland, and Nevada.

The fact that sanitation guidelines do not apply in certain states does not necessarily mean that conditions in these states are worse than the American average. In fact, some of these states are leaders in improving agricultural workers' well-being. Comparing the conditions between the workers who call California home base with those who spend the off-season in the Southeastern states reveals striking differences. In 1993, 49 percent of workers in Southeastern states like Florida did not have ready access to toilets in the fields. This compared to only 11 percent in California. In less than a decade, these conditions had improved, so that 10 percent of workers in the southeastern states and two percent of Californian workers had no access to toilets.

These improvements sound large, but it is still surprising to think that, in the twenty-first century, about one in ten farmworkers in Florida and other parts of the Southeastern United States has no easy access to a toilet during the course of a twelve- to fifteen-hour workday. Imagine a classroom of thirty students in which each day, three pupils had to go without a toilet. If this problem plagued an entire state, society would act quickly to improve the lives of the 10 percent of students who had no access to a toilet.

The pattern for handwashing facilities mirrors that of toilets. In 1993, facilities were not available to 48 percent of farmworkers in Southeastern states, compared to 14 percent in California. The numbers improved so that now nine of every fifty workers in the American Southeast, or 18 percent, have no access to handwashing facilities. In

Fruits like apples are often treated with pesticides.

California, the number has been reduced to three percent. Knowing what we do about the risks of pesticides, the number of people without access to handwashing facilities is still unacceptably high in the American Southeast. It is also worth wondering about the cleanliness of the American food supply when those people who pick the fruits and vegetables Americans consume lack toilets and handwashing facilities. People both within and outside of the fields are having their health needlessly jeopardized by a lack of sanitary facilities.

To make matters worse, growers and labor contractors find ways (both legal and illegal) to get around the laws. For example, the sanitation standards only apply to employers who hired eleven or more workers in "hand labor" on any one day during the previous twelve months. Hand labor is defined as jobs such as hand cultivation, weeding by hand, planting by hand, or packing produce in the fields or in a packing shed. Sometimes employers will hire an entire family, but list only one member on its payroll. The entire earnings of the family are paid to the person on the payroll. So while an employer might have fifty people working for him on any given day, his payroll might show only ten names. It looks like the grower or labor contractor has hired fewer people than he actually has. Consequently, it appears as though the grower need not provide the handwashing and toilet facilities that the law requires for operations of eleven or more people.

infant mortality rate: the rate of infant deaths in a population.

When safeguards are respected, farmworkers are exposed to fewer health risks. Farmworkers who do get sick rarely seek treatment. Medical attention is costly. For illegal migrants, the fear of deportation makes them reluctant to expose themselves to any sort of scrutiny that might draw attention to their illegal status in the United States. As a result, accidents go unreported because illegal migrants do not seek out attention for their injuries. Despite underreporting, evidence points to pesticide exposure, injuries, and illnesses taking a heavy toll. The *infant mortality rate* among migrant workers is twice as high as the American average. Illnesses that plague farmworkers include rashes, eye disease, and chronic pain.

Hunching over in the fields all day causes back injuries, which are especially prevalent among workers who cultivate and harvest crops that grow near the ground. While harvesting things like raspberries, grapes, and apples allows workers to stand straight, other crops, like celery, carrots, and strawberries require that workers bend over for hours a day. Strawberries, particularly infamous for causing serious pain and injury, are known among farm workers as "the devil's fruit." When a farmworker's back hurts too much to work, they are rarely compensated for their injury. Instead, they go home to recuperate without medical care, and hopefully, in a few days they can return to making money in the fields.

Perhaps the most shocking statistic you will ever read about migrant farmworkers is life expectancy. According to Cornell University's "Facts on Farmworkers in the United States," the average life expectancy of a farmworker is only forty-nine years of age! The typical American can expect to live for seventy-five years. Accidents involving transportation to a work site, tractors, and other farm equipment contribute to the low life expectancy.

Children's Plight

overty plays a role in the lack of medical care that farmworkers experience, but poverty's tentacles reach far into other areas, including the lives of migrant children. Poverty draws migrant children into the workforce and away from school. In 1938, most child labor was made illegal, but it was not until 1974, that a law was passed outlawing child labor in the agricultural industry. As it exists today, the law allows for children as young as fourteen to work on farms for unlimited hours outside of school time. Children younger than fourteen are often tolerated and sometimes work alongside their parents outside of school hours. By the time they are sixteen, teens can work in hazardous farm jobs, operating heavy equipment and handling pesticides. In every other American industry, hazardous work can only be undertaken by adults—those workers who are at least eighteen years of age.

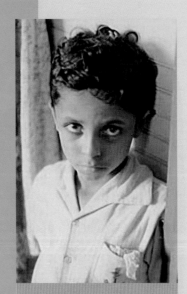

A Latino farmworker's child

oday José is an elderly man. When the back pain from which he suffers mercifully eases—a rare phenomenon these days—his weathered face breaks into a kind smile. But the pain is often so excruciating that he winces when he moves and the lines on his face deepen. José blames much of his pain on the short-handled hoe.

The tool became an early target of farmworker activism. It earned the despised nickname of El Cortito, or the devil's arm. Only twenty-four inches long, workers had to stoop down all day long when tending to crops like lettuce. Working like this led many workers to suffer serious back injuries leading to chronic pain. Injuries were so severe, they could last a lifetime. The California Rural Legal Assistance, an organization of lawyers and others, led a seven-year campaign to rid fields of the short-handled hoe. In 1975, they won. The victory eliminated one of the major causes of chronic back pain.

proficiency: competence in something.

As young as this child is, she is still expected to work in the fields with her parents.

The laws that allow children to work reflect the special place that the family farm holds in American life. But child labor on farms has shifted as the agricultural industry has changed. Today, large corporations own increasing numbers of farms. Fewer local farmers operate relatively small family farms. While some children work for their parents or a local farmer as they once did, many more work as hired labor during seasonal harvests. Other children join the migrant trail with their parents. As Cornell's fact sheet states, "At least one-third of migrant children work on farms to help their families; others may not be hired but are in the fields helping their parents." Concern for the health and well-being of these young workers is increasing in America.

Out of the total number of children who work in the United States, four percent work in agriculture. Yet this four percent is victim to 25 percent of all child workplace deaths. This statistic completely ignores any health-related deaths caused by pesticides, chemicals that are particularly harmful to young people whose immune and neurological systems are still developing. Since the standards of agricultural labor are less stringent than what is generally required in other industries, the circumstances in which children work would often be illegal if they occurred in any other sort of business. Many of the risky jobs that children perform, such as handling dangerous chemicals, would never be allowed legally in a factory.

The risks to their health are not the only risks migrant children face. They also face educational risks. Farm work often draws students out of schools and into the fields. Currently, the average educational level for children of migrant families is sixth grade. This marks a slight improvement from a decade earlier when it was fifth grade. Efforts have been made to keep students in school. For example, during the potato harvest in Maine,

It's hard to know exactly how many children and teens work on farms. According to the National Agricultural Workers Survey, 116,000 fifteen- to seventeen-year-olds worked as hired hands on farms. One shortcoming with this estimate is that it does not take into account fourteen-year-old employees who can be hired legally to work the fields. In addition, the number of children under the age of fourteen working on farms is not documented. Adding to the difficulty of measuring child labor in agriculture is the fact that since the mid-1990s, labor law enforcement has declined. We cannot know the extent of the problem if it is not being measured.

there is no school. This allows children to take part in the harvest without missing school. In spite of these efforts, farmworkers' children have a higher dropout rate than the general population.

The chance to work and earn money is not the only thing that draws migrant children out of the educational system. Migrant children also begin with a disadvantage. In California, 70 percent of migrant students entering kindergarten had low English *proficiency*. By twelfth grade, after nearly a decade and a half in the school system, a whopping 39 percent of these students continued to have low English proficiency. Part of the

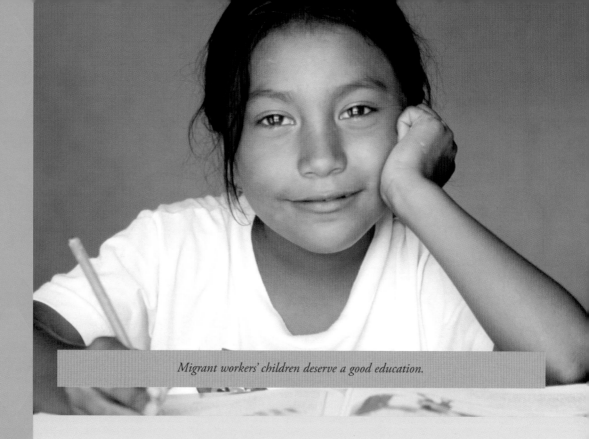

Migrant workers' children deserve a good education.

problem is that migrant children tend to enter the school system later in life. They have the lowest enrollment of any population group. Their dropout rate is twice the national average. They often start school part way through the school year and are forced to leave before the end in order to follow the harvests. When students must move from county to county, state to state, and country to country, the problem is aggravated as they must restart in different systems. Only 10 percent of migrant children reach twelfth grade.

Thankfully, efforts to improve educational opportunities for migrant children are underway. Currently, ten American states interlink with thirty-two Mexican states to provide educational exchanges. The program, called the Migrant Educational Binational Program, deals with the unique educational issues related to students who migrate between the United States and Mexico. It began with California forming an agreement with Mexico and gained steam when the southern border states signed on.

The Migrant Educational Binational Program and other programs like it reduce the educational disruptions felt by migrant children. The U.S. federal government, through the Department of Education's Office of Migrant Education, provides around $300 million a year for programs like summer school for migrant chil- dren, interstate coordination of educational records to make sure that a school has access to a student's history, high school equivalency tests, and other special services designed to help migrant children complete their education.

continuity: consistent; uninterrupted connec- tion.

Education is a key for farmworkers' children to unlock their potential. Efforts to curb the high dropout rate and help stu- dents excel in school are important to achieving educational suc- cess. Today, more migrant children are completing school and even earning university degrees. Changes to the educational sys- tem, however, are not the only thing helping migrant children to succeed.

Farmworkers' families and the broader migrant community also play important roles. Cultural traditions and celebrations among the Latino migrant harvesters remain strong and are important ways for migrant children to feel a sense of stability and *continuity* in their otherwise uprooted lives. A resilient sense of community and the drive for self-betterment inherent in immigrant communities encourages migrant children to achieve things thought nearly impossible only a generation ago. In the next chapter we look at some of the ways that culture and community affect the lives of Latino migrant laborers.

🌀abla 🌀spañol

niño (neen-yo): child

madre (mah-dray): mother

padre (pah-dray): father

estudiantes (ace-too-dee-ont-ays): students

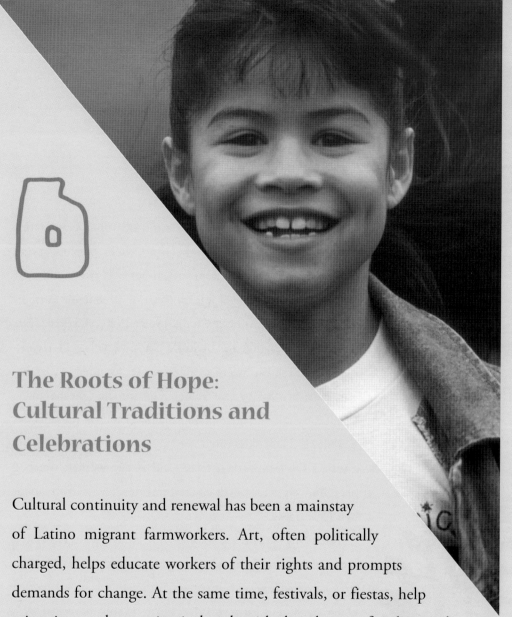

The Roots of Hope: Cultural Traditions and Celebrations

Cultural continuity and renewal has been a mainstay of Latino migrant farmworkers. Art, often politically charged, helps educate workers of their rights and prompts demands for change. At the same time, festivals, or fiestas, help migrating workers maintain bonds with their homes, families, and communities. Since 77 percent of the farmworker population was born in Mexico, cultural celebrations among farmworkers tend to reflect Mexican heritage. Religion also ties the people to their cultural traditions. Together, members of the migrant farmer community find ways to strengthen the ties that bind them. Through support and common experiences, workers find hope and renew their commitment to establishing a better life for themselves and their families.

Migrant workers' rich cultural heritage adds hope to their lives.

Artistic Tradition Among Migrant Farmworkers

Examining the heavy workloads of migrant farmworkers might make you think no art could possibly spring from the fields where the farmworkers labor. However, migrant farmworkers have brought a form of art into the fields. A tradition of protest theater began in the 1960s during the time César Chávez was trying to organize farmworkers. El Teatro Campesino, the Farmworkers Theatre, was founded in Delano, California, in 1967 by Luis Valdez. This traveling theater, made up of farmworkers, performed in the fields and on the sidelines of protests. Their skits often used humor to expose the many injustices the farmworkers faced, and as farmworkers watched the politically motivated entertainment, they learned about their legal rights.

Today, El Teatro Campesino is credited with beginning farmworker theater and creating a new kind of Mexican American drama never before seen. Although it is no longer tied to the UFW, the Farmworkers Theatre is still motivated by a desire for change. Refined on the fields, the Farmworkers Theatre later played for audiences throughout the United States, including a Broadway production and an appearance for the U.S. Senate subcommittee on agriculture. The theater has also had success abroad playing shows in Mexico, Central America, and even Europe.

Theater is not the only form of art that has risen from America's fields. Visual artists have also portrayed the plight of migrant farmworkers in their images. Painter Carlos Almaráz

A traditional Latino dance

alienation: a feeling of being removed from the world around you.

was born in Mexico City and later moved to Los Angeles. He worked for the UFW for three years. His most famous mural encouraged people to take part in the grape boycott. He passed away in 1989, but his work is still shown around the world. Other artists, including Melesio Casas and Consuelo Jimenez Underwood, include migrant workers as subjects of their art. Underwood works with fiber, creating textiles laden with imagery. "Until the border comes down," she says, "I will continue to use barbed wire in my art." In her art, the barbed wire represents not only the border, but the feeling of *alienation* that a person from one culture sometimes feels when trying to adjust to a different one.

Celebrating Culture

Art is not the only way that migrant laborers maintain strong ties to their cultures and communities. Celebrations are other ways for workers to stay connected even when on the migrant trail. Many of the settlements where migrants live have community halls where gatherings can take place. The entire community celebrates some fiestas while others are family affairs.

For migrant workers of Mexican heritage, September 15, Mexico's Independence Day, is an important holiday that is often marked by a community fiesta that includes sports, food, music, and dancing. Children sometimes celebrate by putting on bright dress. Everyone looks forward to later in the evening when children will take turns trying to break the piñata, a papier mâché figure (often in

Piñatas come in various shapes.

the shape of an animal) that is filled with candies or small toys and suspended in the air. The children don blindfolds and take turns swiping at the piñata until it breaks and the goodies inside spill to the ground. Gatherings on September 15 are a time for the community to feel its strength and renew its confidence. Life can be hard as a U.S. migrant farmworker family, but the support of other community members helps the family to believe they can make a better life for themselves and their children.

Just as community celebrations are important among Latino migrant workers, family celebrations are also important. Many migrant workers are forced to spend weeks, months, or even years away from their children and loved ones, so when the opportunity for a family celebration arises, it is a big occasion.

Quinceañeras are elaborate birthday celebrations.

One of the most important family celebrations in Latino culture is *la quinceañera*. Practiced by many different Latino cultures, la quinceañera is a party given by parents for their daughter's fifteenth birthday. The quince (as it is sometimes called; pronounced "keen-say," meaning fifteen) is much more than simply another birthday. Whether the celebration is large or small, it is an important milestone in a young woman's life. It marks the turning point in life from girlhood to womanhood. Historically, the quince signaled that a daughter was now old enough to be married. Today, the meaning has changed somewhat, but the quince still announces the passing of childhood and the beginning of adulthood.

On the day of her quince, a girl wears a special dress. The traditional quinceañera dress is pink, but today white and pastel colors are also popular. The day begins with an important Catholic service for the girl, her immediate family, and her closest friends. During the service, the priest speaks to the girl about what it means to be a woman. After the service, a dinner and dance are held. Up to fifteen boys, known as "chamberlains," and fifteen girls, known as "damas," accompany the young woman and assist in leading

Community parties draw workers together.

the dances and other festivities. The celebration is an exciting time for everyone who takes part, and many girls look forward to their quince for years.

Special celebrations, including the quince, can be a difficult time for workers if they have left their family in Mexico or Central America. Visiting is not as easy as simply getting on a plane and returning home. Workers who leave the United States must repeat the difficult border crossing once they decide to return to American farm fields. For these people, family gatherings and celebrations may be impossible to attend, and keeping in touch through telephone calls and letter-writing is very important. They work with the hope of saving enough money to rescue their families from poverty in their home country or to bring their families to the United States. But making enough money to achieve either of these goals can take a long time. Communities and the support of others help migrant workers who are alone cope with feelings of loss and alienation.

Most Latinos are Roman Catholics.

The Importance of Religion

eligion is a central feature of the lives of migrant farmworkers and the communities they form. Most farmworkers are either Roman Catholic or Protestant, which are both forms of Christianity. Christianity is based on the teachings of Jesus of Nazareth, a Jewish teacher. Roman Catholicism is one of the oldest forms of Christianity and was the religion practiced by most Spaniards when they colonized the Western Hemisphere. Protestantism is the form of Christianity the majority of North Americans practice. Migrant farmworkers usually follow the Roman Catholic faith, although once they arrive in the United States, some convert to Protestantism.

Both Protestant and Roman Catholic agencies work to help migrants keep up their religion. The Catholic Migrant Farmworker Network, for example, provides farmworkers

Images of the Virgin of Guadalupe, Mexico's patron saint, are common at farmworkers' demonstrations. According to tradition, in 1531, the Virgin Mary appeared to Juan Diego, a poor Native farmer, atop a hill near Mexico City. She requested a church be built on that spot. Few believed Juan, and on December 12 he returned to the hill. The Virgin appeared again and told Juan to pick the roses that were now miraculously growing on the wintry hillside, wrap them in his cloak, and bring them to the bishop. Before the bishop, the roses spilled forth, revealing a perfect image of the Virgin emblazoned on Juan's cloak. Today the cloak is still housed in the church that was built on the hillside. Millions of pilgrims trek to pay homage to the Virgin of Guadalupe every year. Over the years, many miracles have been credited to the saint, and she has become a symbol for many causes. She has come to represent the strength of the Catholic Church in the Americas, Mexican nationalism, the movement for Native rights, and the struggle for land reform. In California, the Virgin has become a symbol for the farmworkers' struggle to reform the agricultural industry.

Migrant workers attend church when they are able.

with religious services in the farm fields. This can be important for those who are moving from place to place and have no church they can regularly attend. Taking time to go to church on Sundays, the traditional day of rest in Christian religions, is often not possible. For example, in New York State, the labor law does not mandate that farmworkers be given a day off, so many must work seven days a week.

With such difficult circumstances, community support is crucial for migrant farmworkers to survive. In the face of adversity, the strength and *coherence* of Latino culture has endured. Art, cultural celebrations, and religion are just some of the ways Latino migrant workers hold on to their cultures while building a new culture all their own. In the face of daily struggle and upheaval, connections to their families and cultural history help Latino migrant farmworkers keep their determination and hopes alive.

coherence: logical consistency.

Habla Español

domingo (doe-meen-go): Sunday

iglesia (ee-glay-see-ah): church

hija (ee-ha): daughter

hijo (ee-ho): son

campesino (cahm-pay-see-no): farmworker

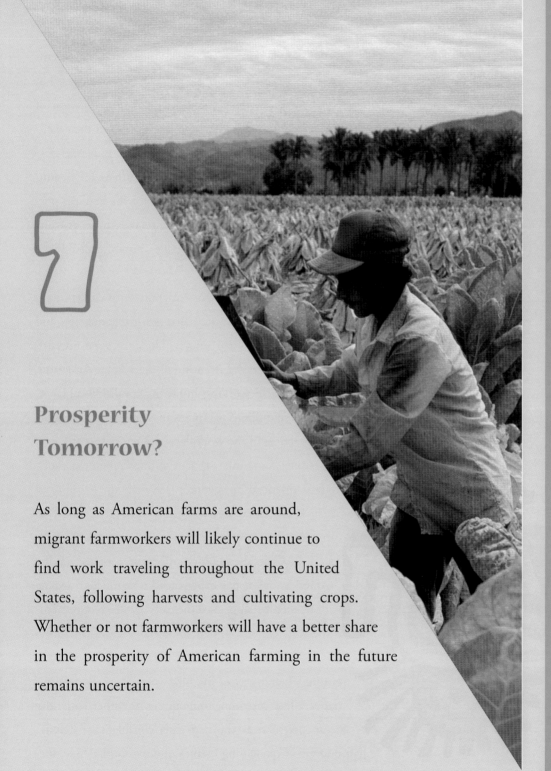

Prosperity
Tomorrow?

As long as American farms are around, migrant farmworkers will likely continue to find work traveling throughout the United States, following harvests and cultivating crops. Whether or not farmworkers will have a better share in the prosperity of American farming in the future remains uncertain.

As long as Americans grow food, they will need someone to pick it.

The question of how farmworkers will adapt to the problems and opportunities with which they are faced can be answered in two ways. Some people might look at the bleak situation of many migrant workers and say that their rights and their well-being will continue to erode, particularly as fewer and larger corporations come to dominate agriculture. Yet others might find the answer is a more positive one. Change for the better is possible so long as consumers, the people who take America's fruits and vegetables home to their dining tables, are informed of the plight of farmworkers.

The past reveals that America's migrant farmworkers have shown an ability to improve their lives with organization and the help of consumers. Their efforts, like the grape boycott, brought their struggle to the attention of the average American. The biggest gains to the working and living conditions of farmworkers came when millions of Americans showed their support for fairer practices in the workplace and refused to buy produce from companies that exploited their workers. Today, American farmworkers have the opportunity to again gain Americans' attention through a variety of means.

While the union movement centered in the American West has experienced a significant decline in its membership since the early 1980s, recent membership has rebounded somewhat. Union membership alone, however, cannot achieve what is necessary to ensure a better way of life for farmworkers. Recent initiatives, like providing migrants with official identity documents such as the matricula consular, are helping halt migrants from sliding further underground. These documents are one way that workers are becoming more visible to the government and the general population. Lack of proper

Migrant workers are striving to improve their future.

Americans need to value individuals who harvest our foods—like the watermelons we eat at summer picnics.

documentation and fear of deportation force workers to hide from authorities and rob workers of the ability to protest unfair treatment. Providing the opportunity for farmworkers to gain legitimate work status also gives them access to their legal rights. By becoming more visible to more people, farmworkers can also encourage American citizens to demand changes to the way that agricultural industries treat their workers.

Some positive change is happening now, but some of the biggest changes are yet to come. Latinos dominate the ranks of migrant farmworkers, and while a massive majority of the 39.9 million Latinos living in the United States do not work as migrant farmworkers, the plight of migrant farmworkers is a very important issue to many in the community. This large segment of the U.S. population is increasingly influential in politics. Much of America's Latino population is composed of young people. In fact, 34.4 percent of Hispanics are under the age of eighteen, the largest proportion of young people of any of America's population groups. As these young people grow and reach voting age, the issues that they identify as important will dominate a larger part of America's political debates. Furthermore, as other groups increase their population at a slower rate, Latinos of voting age will make a larger portion of the total voters in the United States. The abil-

When buying produce be aware of who picked it.

ity to keep the concerns of migrant farmworkers at the forefront of Latino political concerns will remain an important goal in the future.

Latino migrant farmworkers can benefit from a larger Latino population because the issues dear to Latinos in America will come to form a larger part of the country's national debate. Once people are informed about the difficulties migrant farmworkers face, they might begin to make changes about the products they buy in efforts to improve the lives of America's farmworkers. When millions of Americans boycotted major fruit and vegetable companies, they made it known that they supported the rights of farmworkers to demand better wages and working conditions. Today, companies and brands that use workers from the UFW are authorized by the union to put the group's emblem, a black eagle, on their products. These companies and

hen the UFW signs a deal with a food company, they agree to allow the symbol, the black eagle, to appear on the food sold by that company. Many companies like to have the union's symbol on their product because it helps increase sales to people who want to support the union. Therefore, the union gets a labor contract and the company gets good publicity.

the union hope that by putting a union label on their produce, people will make the decision to buy their brand of grapes, oranges, or avocados over the produce of companies who do not hire union workers. Decisions by ordinary consumers, people who buy the fruits and vegetables in grocery stores, can have an impact on the world around them.

Wage increases will likely remain the most important need of migrant farmworkers far into the future. Many consumers support the idea that workers should be paid more and, in fact, are willing to pay a few extra cents for food if they know that money is going to farmworkers. Labor makes up such a small part of the overall cost of food that by raising wages food prices are not increased greatly. According to *Migration News*, only five or six cents of every dollar you spend on produce goes to the workers who planted, cultivated, harvested, and packed that produce. If the average farmworker was given a 40 percent wage increase, the labor costs for a dollar's worth of produce would rise from five or six cents to just seven to nine cents. That means that instead of paying a dollar for a head of lettuce, for example, a consumer would be paying $1.02 or $1.03. Ten dollars of produce would have twenty or thirty cents added on. This may sound like just a few extra cents for consumers, but all those pennies would add up to huge wage increases for farmworkers.

Farmworkers struggle between two worlds. They live in one of the richest countries of the world, the United States, working hard to achieve a better life for themselves and their families. At the same time, they experience a level of poverty unparalleled among the U.S. population. The wealth of American soil has provided a living for countless generations. The wide range of crops that grow throughout its diverse regions continues to allow many people to prosper. Yet farmworkers have not enjoyed the fruits of the land and have experienced declining fortunes over the last several decades. If farmworkers are to prosper today and tomorrow, consumers will have to recognize the responsibility they have in helping farmers to achieve fairer working and living conditions. As consumers, educators, and politicians begin to understand the plight of migrant farmworkers—the people we all depend on for our food—changes will hopefully be made that change this story from one of poverty and toil to one of hope and triumph.

Habla Español

pobreza (po-bray-sah): poverty

esperanza (ace-pair-on-sah): hope

gente (hane-tay): people

Timeline

1846–1848—Mexican-American War.

1845—The United States annexes Texas.

1916—Keating-Owen Act of 1916 passed, first child labor bill (would later be ruled unconstitutional by the U.S. Supreme Court).

March 31, 1927—Labor leader and cofounder of the United Farm Workers of America César Chávez born.

October 24, 1929—"Black Thursday," stock market crashes leading to the Great Depression.

1935—The first Hispanic is elected to the U.S. Senate—Dennis Chávez of New Mexico.

1936—The National Labor Relations Act takes effect.

November 1936—First Social Security number is issued.

1939—John Steinbeck's *Grapes of Wrath* is published. The movies *Gone with the Wind* and *The Wizard of Oz* are released.

1942—The Bracero Program starts between the United States and Mexico; will last until 1964.

March–April 1966—The Peregrinacion (The Pilgrimage), a NFWA-sponsored, 340-mile march of farmworkers from San Francisco to Sacramento.

July 1970—Law forming the Environmental Protection Agency passed.

1973–1975—A UFW-sponsored nationwide boycott of grapes.

1974—Child labor is curtailed in agriculture.

January 14, 1983—Migrant and Seasonal Agricultural Worker Protection Act passes.

January 1, 1994—North American Free Trade Agreement goes into effect.

Further Reading

Ancona, George. *Harvest*. Tarrytown, N.Y.: Marshall Cavendish, 2001.

Ashabranner, Brent, and Paul Conklin. *Dark Harvest: Migrant Farmworkers in America*. Hamden, Conn.: Linnet Books, 1997.

Atkin, S. Beth. *Voices from the Fields: Children of Migrant Farmworkers Tell Their Stories*. Boston, Mass.: Little, Brown, and Company, 2000.

Barger, W. K., and Ernesto M. Reza. *The Farm Labor Movement in the Midwest: Social Change and Adaptation among Migrant Farmworkers*. Austin: University of Texas Press, 1994.

Ferriss, Susan, Ricardo Sandoval, and Diana Hembree. *The Fight in the Fields: Cesar Chavez and the Farmworkers Movement*. Orlando, Fla.: Harcourt Brace & Company, 1997.

Hoyt-Goldsmith, Diane. *Migrant Worker: A Boy from the Rio Grande Valley*. New York: Holiday House, 1996.

Jiménez, Francisco. *La Mariposa*. Boston, Mass.: Houghton Mifflin Company, 1998.

Martinez, Ruben. *Crossing Over: A Mexican Family on the Migrant Trail*. New York: St. Martin's Press, 2001.

Rothenberg, Daniel. *With These Hands: The Hidden World of Migrant Farmworkers Today*. Berkeley and Los Angeles: University of California Press, 1998.

Ryan, Pam Munoz. *Esperanza Rising*. New York: Scholastic Paperbacks, 2002.

Thompson, Charles Dillard, and Melinda Wiggins. *The Human Cost of Food: Farmworkers' Lives, Labor, and Advocacy*. Austin: University of Texas Press, 2002.

For More Information

College Assistance Migrant Program at State University of New York, Oneonta
organizations.oneonta.edu/camp/

Cornell Migrant Program
www.farmworkers.cornell.edu

Farmworkers and Colonia Communities (Homes and Communities)
U.S. Department of Housing and Urban Development
www.hud.gov/groups/farmworkers.cfm

The Farmworkers Website
www.farmworkers.org

Farmworker Justice Fund Inc.
www.fwjustice.org

Geneseo Migrant Center
www.migrant.net

Migation Dialogue
www.migration.ucdavis.edu

The National Agricultural Workers Survey, U.S. Department of Labor,
Office of the Assistant Secretary for Policy
www.dol.gov/asp/programs/agworker/naws.htm

National Association of State Directors of Migrant Education
www.nasdme.org

Student Action with Farmworkers
www.cds.aas.duke.edu/saf/

United Farmworkers Homepage
www.ufw.org

Publisher's note:

The Web sites listed on this page were active at the time of publication. The publisher is not responsible
for Web sites that have changed their addresses or discontinued operation since the date of publication. The
publisher will review the Web sites and update the list upon each reprint.

Index

Picture Credits

Benjamin Stewart: pp. 17, 54, 55, 56, 62, 74, 88, 89, 96

Centro Library and Archives, Ceentro de Estudios Puertorriqueños, Hunter College, CUNY, Photographer unknown: pp. 53

Charles A. Hack: p. 93

Gerardo Rizo: p. 94

PhotoDisc: p. 65

Photos.com: pp. 9, 11, 12, 15, 19, 44, 57, 66, 70, 73, 78, 84, 87, 91, 92, 99, 100, 101, 102, 103

Library of Congress: pp. 21, 24, 27, 29, 45, 69, 80, 82,

The Records of the Offices of the Government of Puerto Rico in the U.S., Centro de Estudios Puertorriqueños, Hunter College, CUNY, Photographer Unknown: pp. 31, 32, 35, 36, 38, 46, 64

Biographies

Christopher Hovius is a graduate of Queen's University at Kingston, Ontario. He currently lives in Toronto, Ontario, where he is earning his law degree and working as a freelance writer.

Dr. José E. Limón is professor of Mexican-American Studies at the University of Texas at Austin, where he has taught for twenty-five years. He has authored over forty articles and three books on Latino cultural studies and history. He lectures widely to academic audiences, civic groups, and K–12 educators.